Anna and The Hermitage CATS

Mary Ann Allin
and
Maria Haltunen

Illustrated
by
Anatoly Belkin
and
Maryana Sokolinskaya

A Letter from the Hermitage Museum Director

Dear Young Readers,

When I was a boy, I explored the treasures of the State Hermitage Museum nearly every day. My father, you see, was the director of this wonderful museum, which occupies six magnificent buildings along the Neva River in St. Petersburg, Russia.

My favorite game was to hide among the gigantic suits of armor and pretend to be a knight on a big white horse. I also liked to watch the famous Peacock Clock and wait for the special day when a curator would come with the key, wind the mechanism, and set the clock parts moving.

In my childhood, I discovered the secret world of the Hermitage cats. Along the underground hallways and in the attics and courtyards of the museum buildings, the cats patrol for mice.

Cats have been a feature of the Hermitage for more than 250 years, when it was the residence of the Russian tsars. In those days the "Winter Palace Cats," as they were called, were all the same kind — Russian Blues — very big and very good mousers. Now we have all kinds of cats — all sizes, all colors, all ages.

At the Hermitage Museum we take good care of our cats. We provide food and water, and we invite veterinarians to give them check-ups. Our cats are an important part of our museum "family" and — who knows? — maybe they take an interest in the art.

In spring we often have a Day of the Cats. Children enjoy this day, and the cats do, too. We have exhibitions for everyone, including exhibitions for the cats. Children bring drawings and photographs of cats, and the best are displayed.

When you finish this story about Anna and the Hermitage cats, you may want to draw a picture of a cat or imagine an adventure discovering the great art at the Hermitage. An art museum is a place where children and their parents can discover many unexpected things, even cats.

M. B. Piotrovsky

The State Hermitage Museum in St. Petersburg has more than one thousand rooms and three million works of art. It is home to nearly 17,000 paintings, 12,500 sculptures, and 50 cats. Several million people visit the museum each year. They admire two famous Madonnas painted by Leonardo da Vinci, and they gaze at Michelangelo's sculpture called *The Crouching Boy.*

The cats live in their own underground world. They play, nap, and catch mice in the Hermitage basement. Most visitors do not see them.

Anna knew all this, the day she visited the museum. More than the Madonnas by Leonardo or the Michelangelo sculpture, she wanted to see the cats. And she wanted to find one — a special one — to draw.

Anna loved to draw cats — fat cats,
skinny cats, scruffy cats, smooth cats.
So one sunny day when the ice flowed on the
Neva River, Anna packed up her sketchbook
and pencils and paid a visit to the
Hermitage Museum.

Anna

marched through

the museum's

huge iron gate.

She headed straight for
the Museum Director's office.

"May I draw one of your cats?" Anna asked.

The director looked surprised.
"Do you mean a cat in one of our paintings?"
he asked.

"No," said Anna. "I mean a real live cat —
a cat that lives in the museum."

"But we have many cats," said the director.
"How will you know which one to draw?"

Anna smiled. "I will know."

The director smiled, too. "Many artists have
created pictures of cats, but you will be
the first to draw a Hermitage cat."

He called to Masha in the next room.

A moment later,

a tall woman with a kind face walked in.

"Masha is

Press Secretary to the Cats,"

said the director.

"She can help you find them."

Masha and Anna
entered a long hallway.

"We'll be very quiet and
look carefully," she said.
"The Hermitage cats are
rather shy and like to hide."

Anna looked for
a hint of whisker,
a wisp of tail —
but saw nothing.

They stepped into
the Ancient Egypt Room.

"The Egyptians loved cats,"
said Masha.

"I think I see a cat figurine,"
said Anna.

But she saw
     no
          real
              live
                    cats.

In the next gallery, a woman sat
in a chair beneath a work of art.

The woman smiled at Anna and
Masha. "This is an interesting
painting. It is called
Peasant Woman with a Cat."

"She must love her cat," said
Masha. "See how she wraps
it up like a baby? And it looks
like she is feeding it
a spoonful of honey.
Perhaps the cat has
caught a cold."

nna thought about the painting. Then she looked around the large room. "Cats like cozy places," she said slowly. "Maybe we won't find real

live

cats

in the galleries."

asha smiled. "I think you are right, Anna. Look out this window and tell me what you see."

Anna climbed up on a bench. She looked into the courtyard far below. "Look, Masha!" she cried. "Paw prints in the snow!"

The paw prints led to the museum's basement door. Now Anna knew what to do. They had to go down as far as they could go.

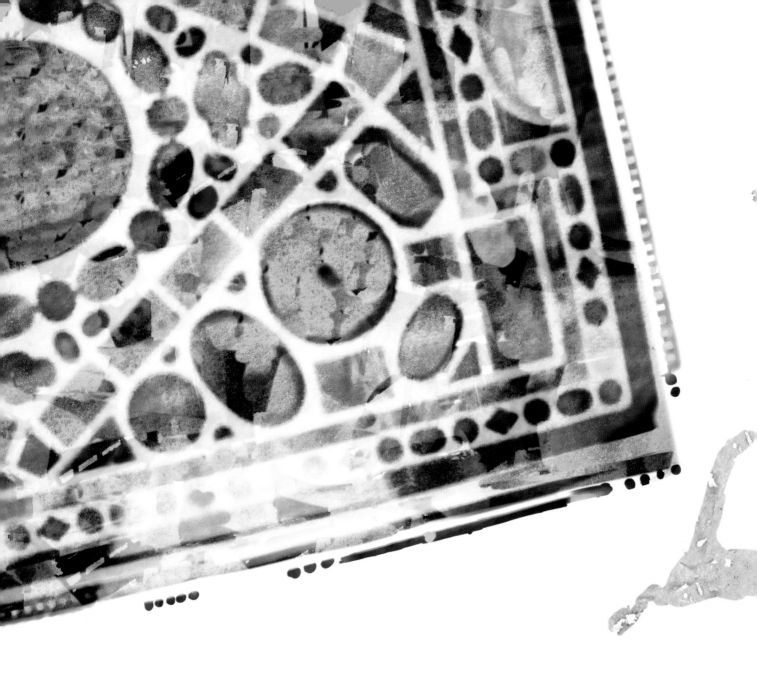

Anna and Masha went through many more rooms of the museum.

They passed paintings, sculptures, and objects decorated with colorful stones.

nna stopped for just a moment and pointed to the Peacock Clock in its glass case. She wanted to touch a nearby table decorated with many colored stones — blue lapis, green malachite, and smooth round golden shapes.

Masha said, "The yellow pieces are not the same as stones. They are called amber. In some you see insects or plant leaves that are many centuries old. Amber brings good luck."

"Amber is beautiful," Anna repeated the new word slowly, "like the color of the sun."

They continued along corridors,

    down the Jordan Staircase —

        down,

           down,

              down.

"Will I have good luck now?" asked Anna.
    "Will we find the real cats soon?"

        "Let's go down here," said Masha.
          She pointed to the basement entrance.
           The two went

             down,

               down,

                 down

                   to a dim
                       underground
                     world.

Anna whispered, "The cats."
She looked up at the soft shapes and
big eyes on the overhead heating
pipes. "Why are the pipes wrapped
in cloth?" asked Anna.

"To make a soft warm place for cats
to sleep," explained Masha.

"Or to watch for mice!" said Anna
with excitement.

They came to a wide passage stacked with
cardboard boxes. Some boxes had doors and
curtained windows, like a cat apartment house.
All sorts of cats lived here in the basement
of the museum, and Masha knew each one of them.

"This is Renoir," Masha stroked a nearby cat.

"And that little one is Van Dyke.

Over there is Stripes.

And where is Naughty Red-Ears?...

Have you seen the one you want to draw?" asked Masha.

Anna shook her head, "Not yet."

asha and Anna
stepped into
a nearby office
full of busy people.
"Look!" cried Anna.
"More cats!"

A whiskery cat with gray
eyes peered up at Anna.
It looked like Naughty
Red-Ears, sitting very
still and staring at her
from behind a plant.
Anna was not sure
she wanted to draw
a naughty cat.

have one more room to show you." Masha led Anna to a workshop full of old carriages and furniture. On the other side of the room, a carpenter looked up from his work.

"Hello!" Anna called out. "Are any cats hiding in here?"

"No," answered the carpenter. "But if you peek inside that royal carriage, you'll see a velvet cushion. That cushion belonged to the cat of a Russian princess."

Anna opened the carriage door and peeked inside. It was very dusty.

"Ker-choo!" she sneezed.

"Ker-choo!" came a tiny sneeze in reply.

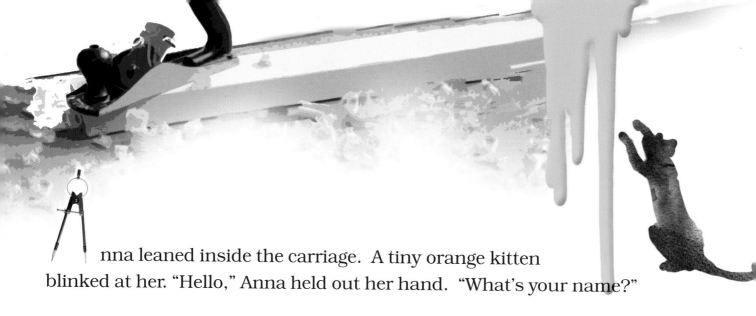

nna leaned inside the carriage. A tiny orange kitten blinked at her. "Hello," Anna held out her hand. "What's your name?"

"Why, I've never seen that kitten before," Masha said.
"Would you like to name her?"

"She's the color of the golden shapes in the table upstairs," said Anna, "and it's good luck that we found her. Let's name her Amber."

"Welcome to the Hermitage, little Amber," said Masha, and she lifted the kitten gently onto the red velvet cushion.

Quickly Anna opened her sketchbook. At last she had found the perfect cat to draw.

The carpenter smiled his approval. "Little Amber it is! She's a royal princess, all right. The other cats like to hide down here in the basement, but this cat," he chuckled, "this little one acts as if she belongs in all the rooms of a palace museum."

Carefully Anna drew the last whisker and showed the picture to Masha and the carpenter.

"Very good!" they agreed.

"May I leave my picture with Amber and the other cats?" asked Anna.
"It will be their own cat portrait."

"I know just the place," said Masha. "We will hang the drawing close to the cat
apartment house. You can see your picture the next time you visit Amber."

"Yes," said Anna, noticing that Stripes and Naughty Red-Ears were the first to get a
close look at the new portrait of Amber. "And maybe I can draw the other cats, too."

Masha laughed. "Soon the cats will have as many fine pictures downstairs as the
museum has upstairs."

Amber purred contentedly as she drifted off to sleep.

Upstairs in the Hermitage Museum, you can see the art objects
and paintings that Anna discovered while searching for the perfect
cat to draw on a sunny day when the ice flowed on the Neva River.

Cat figurine
Egypt, 1000 BC
Bronze with gold inlays

Leonardo da Vinci
(1452–1519)
Madonna and Child
Italy, 1490s
Tempera on canvas

David Ryckaert III
(1612–1661)
Peasant Woman with a Cat
Flanders, early 1640s
Oil on canvas